A NOTE TO PARENTS

Reading Aloud with Your Child
Research shows that reading books aloud is the single most valuable support parents can provide in helping children learn to read.
- Be a ham! The more enthusiasm you display, the more your child will enjoy the book.
- Run your finger underneath the words as you read to signal that the print carries the story.
- Leave time for examining the illustrations more closely; encourage your child to find things in the pictures.
- Invite your youngster to join in whenever there's a repeated phrase in the text.
- Link up events in the book with similar events in your child's life.
- If your child asks a question, stop and answer it. The book can be a means to learning more about your child's thoughts.

Listening to Your Child Read Aloud
The support of your attention and praise is absolutely crucial to your child's continuing efforts to learn to read.
- If your child is learning to read and asks for a word, give it immediately so that the meaning of the story is not interrupted. DO NOT ask your child to sound out the word.
- On the other hand, if your child initiates the act of sounding out, don't intervene.
- If your child is reading along and makes what is called a miscue, listen for the sense of the miscue. If the word "road" is substituted for the word "street," for instance, no meaning is lost. Don't stop the reading for a correction.
- If the miscue makes no sense (for example, "horse" for "house"), ask your child to reread the sentence because you're not sure you understand what's just been read.
- Above all else, enjoy your child's growing command of print and make sure you give lots of praise. *You are your child's first teacher — and the most important one. Praise from you is critical for further risk-taking and learning.*

— Priscilla Lynch
Ph.D., New York University
Educational Consultant

P9-DEW-086

To Rachel

CIP information available upon request.

ISBN 0-590-53951-5

12 11 10 9 8 7 6 5 4 3 2 1   9   5 6 7 8 9/9 0/0

Printed in the U.S.A.

Monster Manners

by Joanna Cole
Illustrated by Jared Lee

Hello Reader! — Level 3

SCHOLASTIC INC.
New York Toronto London Auckland Sydney

Rosie Monster looked like
a perfect little monster.
She had nice strong teeth,
and sharp little claws,
and green eyes that
glowed in the dark.

Rosie had just one problem.
She was always forgetting
her monster manners.

Monsters are supposed

to fight with their friends

and break each other's toys.

Rosie played nicely with everyone.

This made her mother very unhappy.

Monsters are supposed

to growl loudly

when they answer the telephone.

Rosie always forgot
and said "Hello"
in a polite voice.

Her father found this very upsetting.

Monsters are supposed

to chew up rocks

to show how fierce they are.

After one bite,

Rosie would stop crunching

and run for her toothbrush.

She didn't like the way

the bits of rock got stuck

between her teeth.

One day, when the family
was out walking,
Rosie even helped an old man
cross the street.

Her mother and father
shook their heads.
"I'm afraid Rosie will
never learn," said her father.
"How will she get along
in the world?" asked her mother.

While they were talking,

Rosie's best friend, Prunella, came by.

"You have good manners, Prunella,"
said Rosie. "Will you teach me?"
"Sure," said Prunella.

And so Prunella came over

to give Rosie some lessons.

The first lesson was making

monster faces.

Prunella showed Rosie
how to make
Monster Face
Number One . . .

Monster Face
Number Two . . .

Monster Face
Number Three . . .

and Monster Face
Number Four.

Then it was Rosie's turn.

She tried Monster Face Number One,

then Number Two . . .   Number Three . . .

and Number Four.

"That's terrible," said Prunella.

"Let's try something else.

Maybe you're better at table manners."

Prunella took Rosie

to a restaurant

and ordered lunch.

Everyone fainted when
Prunella started to eat.
What a horrible sight!

Rosie forgot
her monster manners,
as usual.
She used her napkin,
and her fork and spoon.
And when she asked
Prunella to pass the salt,
she forgot again
and said "Please."

Prunella was angry.

"You're not even trying,"

she said.

Prunella decided to give Rosie
one more chance.

"This time we will practice our
visiting manners," she said.

"We'll drop in on my uncle Ned."

Prunella behaved perfectly

for a monster.

First she rang the doorbell

ten times without stopping —

even when she heard her uncle say,

"Come in."

Then Prunella knocked so hard

the door fell down.

She went inside

and jumped up and down

on her uncle's favorite chair.

She spilled a vase

of flowers on the rug.

And finally she stepped
very hard
on Uncle Ned's foot.
Uncle Ned was
proud of Prunella.

But Rosie said,

"How do you do?"

and sat quietly on the sofa.

Uncle Ned was horrified.

He asked Prunella

to take her friend home

until she could learn

better manners.

Prunella threw up her hands.

"I did my best, Rosie,"

she said.

"I can't do any more."

Rosie hung her head
and followed Prunella.
For the first time,
Rosie realized how unhappy
she had made everyone.
And now she felt unhappy, too.

When Rosie and Prunella
got to the Monsters' house,
they saw a big mess.
A pipe had broken
and water was pouring
everywhere.

"Help!" cried Rosie.

"We're getting flooded."

Rosie's mother and father

came running.

Rosie's mother called the plumber
and growled into the phone.
The plumber hung up.

Rosie's father called and
roared into the phone.
The plumber hung up harder.

Prunella tried, too,

but the same thing happened.

They were getting nowhere,

and the water was getting deeper.

Something had to be done.

And Rosie did it.

Without thinking,

she dialed the phone

and said in a nice voice,

"Hello. We have a leak

at the Monsters' house.

Can you come over, please?"

"I'll be right there,"
said the plumber.
"Thank you," said Rosie.

After the plumber had left

and everything was back

to normal,

Rosie's mother turned

to Rosie's father.

"You know, dear," she said,
"Rosie's strange manners
do come in handy sometimes."

"We're lucky to have her,"

said Rosie's father,

"strange manners and all."

They gave Rosie

a hug and a kiss

and sent her out to play.

"Mind your manners, dear,"
called Rosie's mother
from the window.

"I will, Mother,"
answered Rosie.

About the Author

Joanna Cole has written more than fifty books for children. She is the widely acclaimed author of *The Magic School Bus* series, as well as the *Clown-Around* series; *How You Were Born*; and *Who Put the Pepper in the Pot?* Ms. Cole lives in Connecticut with her husband and daughter.

About the Illustrator

Jared Lee has illustrated dozens of children's books, including *The Teacher from the Black Lagoon* series. He lives in Lebanon, Ohio, with his wife P.J., dogs, ponies, cats, and ducks.